KU-719-787

Schools Library and Information Services

S00000648761

For Jinx, with love P G
For Genny C J C

© 2003 The Chicken House
Text © 2003 Pippa Goodhart
Illustrations © 2003 Caroline Jayne Church

First published in the United Kingdom in 2003 by
The Chicken House, 2 Palmer Street, Frome, Somerset, BA11 1DS

All rights reserved.
No part of this publication may be reproduced or
transmitted or utilized in any form or by any means,
electronic, mechanical, photocopying or otherwise,
without the prior permission of the publisher.

The moral rights of the author and illustrator have been asserted.

Printed and bound in Singapore

British Library Cataloguing in Publication Data available.

HB   ISBN: 1 903434 78 5
PB   ISBN: 1 904442 02 1

Pudding

Will You Be My Friend?

L -46640

648761	SCH
	Jy900

By Pippa Goodhart

Illustrated by Caroline Jayne Church

The
Chicken HOUSE

This is Pudding . . .

Nobody plays with Pudding . . .

. . . and nobody plays with Lucy.

So they are sad . . .

. . . and then Pudding is bad.

So he runs away . . .

. . . all on his own . . .

. . . . until he finds Lucy.

. . . and Pudding licks Lucy.

So they play together . . .

. . . and they stay together.

Forever.